JPIC Ravish
Ravishankar, Anushka
The boy who drew cats

$9.95
ocn879677610
Second Reprint. 07/11/2014

THE BOY WHO DREW CATS

Anushka Ravishankar
Christine Kastl

Akiro drew cats. Now there's nothing wrong with drawing cats. Lots of people draw cats, but Akiro was different. He drew only cats. Nothing but cats. No dogs, no horses, no houses, mountains, flowers, or people - only cats. In fact, he drew them all the time.

His brothers and sisters helped their parents as they worked in the fields. But Akiro sat at the edge of the field, drawing cats in the wet mud.

After a day's work, everyone ate their rice and fish hungrily. But Akiro drew cats in the rice and tried to coax them to eat the fish. And when the cats did not eat the fish, he wept and refused to have his supper.

His mother was fed up. His father was in despair.

'What do we do with the boy?' they asked each other. They could not understand this quiet son of theirs who had started drawing cats as soon as he was old enough to draw.

'Why do you draw cats all the time?' his mother asked him one day.

'You see, Mother,' Akiro told her solemnly, 'I have to keep practicing until I draw the perfect cat.'

'And what is the perfect cat?'

'I don't know,' Akiro replied, frowning with thought. 'But it's not this.' And he wiped out the cat he had drawn in the mud.

'Looks like a perfectly good cat to me,' his mother sighed, shaking her head and wondering what would become of her odd little boy.

Finally, Akiro's parents decided to send him to a nearby temple to study under the priest there.

'He's not made for the fields and farming,' said his father.

'Maybe he'll become a learned priest,' said his mother.

At the temple, the students learnt to make ink, to dip their brush in the ink, and to write with the brush. But Akiro dipped his brush in the ink and drew cats. When he was asked to write a word, he drew a cat. When he was asked to do a sum, he drew a cat.

Then one day, when everyone was taking an afternoon nap, he drew cats on all the rice paper screens in the temple.

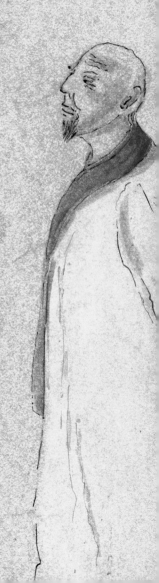

The old priest looked at his beautiful screens,
now covered with cats, and sighed. He called
Akiro to him.

'Akiro, Akiro, you cannot become a priest,' he
said. 'You do not have the temperament.'

Akiro did not know what a temperament was,
but he realized that he was being told to leave.

'Do you have any advice for me before I leave?' Akiro asked the priest.

The priest did not know what to say. Suddenly the words came out of his mouth, straight from his heart, without passing through his mind: 'Stay away from large places. Sleep only in small spaces.'

Akiro was puzzled. It was strange sort of advice for a priest to give his student when he was sending him away into the world. But a teacher's advice has to be taken with gratitude, even when it sounds odd and meaningless. So Akiro bowed low and left.

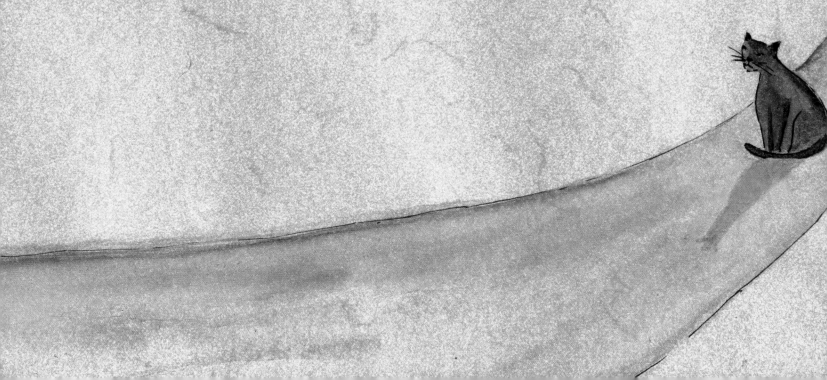

He wandered around for half a day, not knowing where to go. Then he remembered that there was a large temple in the neighboring village.

'They might need a student to help them keep the temple clean,' he thought and walked quickly towards the village. It was almost night-time when he reached.

Akiro went to the temple. It was open, but it was dark and silent inside. 'Anybody there?' called Akiro. There was no answer.

He stepped into the temple and stood there while his eyes got used to the darkness. A single lamp was burning in the temple, and it threw a ghostly light on the white rice paper screens that stood on all four sides of the room. In a corner were a brush, an ink stick, and a hollow stone with a bit of water in it.

A very strange feeling came over Akiro. As if in a dream, he went over to the corner, dipped the ink stick in the water, and rubbed it on the stone to make ink. He dipped the brush into the ink. And then he began to draw cats. Akiro had drawn cats for years. He could draw cats with his eyes shut.

In the gloom of the temple, he could barely see what he was doing, and yet, somehow, Akiro knew that the cats he drew on those rice paper screens were perfect. He could almost hear them purr.

By the time he had filled all the screens with cats, Akiro was so tired, he was tottering on his feet. He was about to drop down on to the floor to sleep when he heard the old priest's voice in his head: 'Stay away from large places. Sleep only in small spaces.'

In one corner of the large room, he saw a little cupboard.
It was dusty and musty, but it was small. He got in and
shut the door tight behind him. Akiro was so tired that he
fell asleep at once.

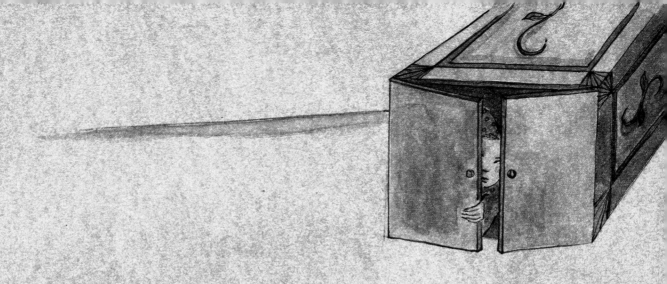

But suddenly, in the middle of the night, he woke up with a start. Someone or something was screeching loudly. Frightened, Akiro closed his eyes, pushed his fingers in his ears and rolled up into a tight little ball in the cupboard.

He fell asleep again, and when he awoke, the sunlight was streaming cheerfully in through the slats in the cupboard door.

'What a terrible dream that was!' he mumbled to himself, rubbing his eyes sleepily, as he tumbled out of the cupboard. The sight he saw made him gasp.

In the middle of the room, lying on the floor was a gigantic goblin rat. It was dead.

Akiro stood frozen for a few moments, and then he remembered the noises of the night. Slowly, his eyes moved upwards towards the rice paper screens. One by one he looked at the cats – the perfect cats – that he had drawn at night. Every one of the cats had blood on its face.

He had barely understood what had happened when a huge crowd of people came into the temple, led by the priest of the temple.

'There he is!' they called out. 'The boy who killed the goblin!'

Before Akiro knew it, he had been taken to the priest's home and given so much to eat and drink that he could barely walk.

'You are our savior!' said the priest of the big temple to Akiro. 'Long ago, in a dream, I was told that the temple could only be saved by a boy who drew cats. I thought it was the usual silliness of dreams. But still, I left a lamp and a brush and ink in the temple every night. And now here you are! You have killed the goblin rat which has haunted the temple for years! If you will stay and be my student, I will make you the head priest of the temple when you grow up.'

But Akiro shook his head and smiled. 'I do not have the temperament,' he said.

So the people of the village gave him money and gifts, and escorted him home to his parents who were very happy to see him.

Over the years, Akiro roamed across the world,
drawing cats wherever he went.

When he grew up he became a very famous
artist, and though he grew quite old, he was
always known as the boy who drew cats.

The Boy Who Drew Cats

© and ℗ 2008 Karadi Tales Company Pvt. Ltd.
Second Reprint 2013

Text: Anushka Ravishankar
Illustrations: Christine Kastl

Karadi Tales Company Pvt. Ltd.
3A Dev Regency 11 First Main Road Gandhinagar Adyar Chennai 600020
Ph: +91 44 4205 4243 Email: contact@karaditales.com
Website: www.karaditales.com

Distributed in North America by Consortium Book Sales & Distribution
The Keg House 34 Thirteenth Avenue NE Suite 101 Minneapolis MN 55413-1006 USA
Orders: (+1) 731-423-1550 orderentry@perseusbooks.com
Electronic ordering via PUBNET (SAN 631760X) Website: www.cbsd.com

Printed in India
ISBN 978-81-8190-159-0